STORIES FROM THE FRINGE

By J.R. Roper

STORIES FROM THE FRINGE

By J.R. Roper

HIDDEN COTTAGE
PRESS

Published by Hidden Cottage Press

Cover art by Luke Spooner of Carrion House

TABLE OF CONTENTS

For my better half.

Of the Lake

Jay looked over the lake, a pane of silver reflecting the heavens. He'd always avoided such places. The idea of slowing down had been driven out of him long ago. But where had the habit of industry gotten him? It had kept him single, that was certain. After turning off his cell phone for the last time and tossing it onto the couch, he rested his head on the cushion of a cozy chair; a cup of coffee steamed in his hand.

Cool air blew through an open window and mingled with the heavy scent of cedar. The stillness of the lake seemed absurd. So much life teemed below, yet on the surface, all was calm. Until a ripple spread from the end of his dock.

Jay leaned forward, placing his coffee cup on the side table. The boat he'd rented sat near the disturbance. Shaking his head, he rubbed his eyes. When he opened them, a dark figure stood on the dock's end, as if it had risen from the water.

He turned off the light next to his chair and moved

closer to the window. The person lifted a pale arm and motioned, as if inviting someone. From the look of the arm, it was a woman. He took his flask from the side table and added some Old Grand-Dad to his coffee.

Jay took a drink and glanced out the window again. The woman looked in his direction. Was she smiling? Her blue eyes glowed against her pale skin and the landscape of gray water. He grabbed the flask, took a long swig, and made for the door. Once in his sandals, he paused as he gripped the door handle. He'd simply tell her to leave and be done with it. It was his dock, after all.

After a deep breath, he switched on the exterior light and stepped outside. "Who are you? What do you want?" He moved closer, stepping onto the dock, creaking across the weathered planks.

"No, Mr. Dever. Who are you?" Her voice was soft and soothing. She sat on the edge of the dock.

He stood for a moment. The lake seemed even more silent than before. Was she another vacationer, someone who'd simply strolled onto his dock? Or was she one of the owners, or a worker perhaps, who favored the view from here?

"Why are you on my dock?" It came out harsher than he meant.

"Your dock?" She raised her hand and waved him

forward. "I've been here, alone, for far too long."

It felt more like a command than an invitation. He stopped just short of her reach, fresh air brushing his face; the only proof time hadn't stopped.

"Sit next to me." She sounded like the breeze itself.

It couldn't hurt to join her. Jay crouched and sat cross-legged.

Her black dress dangled in the water around her white feet. Her head was covered by a wavering black cloth that made her nose and the curl of her lips barely visible.

"You can't relax with your feet tangled." Wild black curls surrounded her fair face as she took his outside foot and slowly extended his leg, removing his sandal. Then, with just as much grace, did the same to the other. The water enveloped his feet and ankles, cold and numbing.

"What's your name?" he asked. The question felt just as awkward as normal.

She smiled. A kind and gracious smile. "I hope you discover it."

Eddie, his asshole friend. He'd set this up. "Who put you up to this?"

She gently caressed his hand. "You're inquisitive. I like that."

Jay jerked his hand away. "Eddie put you up to

this, didn't he? If he's paying by the minute, you might as well leave now." His face heated like a furnace. He didn't mean it, even if Eddie had hired her.

"No one paid me to meet with you." She reached inside her shawl and pulled out a black orb, the size of a ping-pong ball, attached to a silver chain. "I've come to offer you this." She looked to the sky. "Isn't it amazing?"

Eddie had tried too hard with this one. Jay inched away.

"Haven't you ever wondered about what's beyond the sky?"

"Not really."

She brushed his cheek with the back of her hand. "I'll leave our next meeting up to you." Her outstretched hand held the orb in front of him, as if offering a gift.

Jay looked past it.

She placed it back in her shawl and grasped his arm, pulling him toward her. A soft hand tilted his head onto her shoulder. She smelled like crisp night air.

Song drifted from her lips, words he didn't understand.

Jay's eyes felt heavy. Her voice traveled from his ears and into his veins. Muscles relaxed after years of tension. Everything became foggy, and the world faded away.

———

THE EARLY SUN'S LIGHT CREPT ACROSS HIS FACE, inviting him to wake. Jay sat up in the recliner and looked out the window. Whitecaps rolled onto shore. The dock was empty, as was the flask next to his chair. The smile he awoke with vanished. Like so many women before, she'd been a phantom of his dreams.

Jay started a pot of coffee—his only source of real happiness, at times. He had two more days in this cabin, but thought tonight might be the night. He went into the bedroom and stared at his suitcase.

A rich scent filled the air as the coffee dripped. He sat in silence, until it beeped. Grinning once again, he poured himself a large cup. A deep swallow flooded his body with warmth. He walked to the door and stepped into his sandals, placed exactly where he remembered them from his dream.

A stiff breeze blew through his hair as he looked to the end of the dock, hoping that someone might be seated there. He strolled down the rugged steps onto its gray planks. The waves lashed against the dock, causing his boat to bump into the old tires that hung from the posts. He went to the end and sat, just as he'd done before. He removed his sandals and placed his feet in the lake, water splashing up onto his legs.

He sat for an hour, watching the sky grow from blue to an almost threatening overcast. A loud storm would be perfect this night. He looked into his empty coffee cup, knowing he should do the right thing and at least finish the pot. Something grabbed his attention in the water as he went to stand.

Peering over the side of the dock, he saw something round that glinted through the unruly waves. *It wasn't a dream?* His neck nettled as he stared at the orb. Sucking in a breath, he slipped into the water, the chill prickling his skin as he dove for the orb. There it was, attached to a thin silver chain. Jay plucked it from the sandy lake bottom. From it, heat traveled down his arm and into his body. He felt it surround him, a blanket of protection from the lake's stinging cold.

Pale hands clasped over his hand and the orb, and black locks of hair ensnared him. Jay's throat squeezed with airless panic as he stared into blue eyes.

DEEP BELOW

Stephanie pulled up to 105 West Drive, a white two-story, wrapped with a brightly painted front porch. Fully bloomed daffodils lined the front walk. Though she'd never been there before, the place reminded her of her grandparents' old house.

She parked on the street and locked her doors as she got out, a habit not necessary in the area, but one ingrained since attending college. Her mom had found the place in the local rental section—an old couple with an extra room. It was the perfect solution for her. She needed to be on her own, but also, as her mother delicately put it, needed someone to look after her.

Stephanie knocked on the front door. Moments later, a thin elderly woman with tightly permed hair peeked through the window, smiled, and opened the door.

"You must be Stephanie."

"That's me." She tried to pull her gaze from the woman's eyes, but her blue irises seemed as deep as the

7

ocean, and her eyelids were rimmed in red sadness.

"Please, come in." The woman opened the door wider and placed a hand on Stephanie's shoulder. "My name is Cora. Jim, my husband, is in town and should be back soon. He's looking forward to meeting you." Cora gave Stephanie's upper arm a light squeeze and led the way in.

Stephanie hesitated before entering. Maybe Cora was the touchy-feely type. Scents of lemon cleaning spray and hundred-year-old dust battled it out in the entry room, a large empty space, with an area rug in the center and doors leading off in three directions. To the right, a wooden spiral staircase.

"Your room is on the second floor." Cora led her up the wooden staircase at an easy pace, while complaining about her aching hips. Reaching the top, she sighed and motioned to the door before them. "First door on the right. Here we are."

The room had a brass princess bed covered by a yellow quilt, white curtains stretching from ceiling to floor over the lone window, and a faded, flowery pattern covering the walls. The furniture was adequate, with a desk in the corner, a large wardrobe for her clothes, and a nightstand.

"This was my daughter's room." Cora half smiled. "I'll let you settle in. Care for some tea or coffee in a bit?"

"Sounds nice." Stephanie strode to the bed and sat on the comforter, staring hard at the floor and hoping to be left alone.

Cora loitered in the doorway for a moment, before slinking away without another word.

After a few trips to her car, Stephanie unloaded all her belongings, refolded and hung her clothes, plugged in her laptop, and hoped they actually had wireless internet like they'd promised. Her network search immediately pulled up *Nelson House*, but she didn't know the password.

A knock at the door.

"Hello?"

"Come down for something to drink. Jim's home."

Not wanting to start out on the wrong foot, Stephanie followed Cora down the stairs and into the dining room, which was located directly across from the staircase.

Jim was seated and reading the newspaper. He folded it in half and stood. "Pleased to meet you."

"Likewise." Stephanie walked over and shook his hand. Jim's eyes were as blue as Cora's, but they held no sadness, rather, a genuine happiness, as if the eyes themselves were smiling.

Cora looked away and entered a hallway on the other side of the room. Stephanie's gaze followed her out.

"Don't mind her," Jim said. "Just has a hard time with new lodgers. Hates seeing the old ones go, you see. And she already likes you enough to know she'll miss you when you leave."

"Well," Stephanie pushed her hair out of her face, "I don't intend to leave any time soon."

Jim shook his head. "No. I'm sure not. Settled in then?"

Cora placed a tray on the table with small white teacups, a wooden box filled with a variety of teas, and small containers of sugar cubes and creamer.

Stephanie sat next to Jim and poured herself some hot water. She chose a mint-flavored green tea and let it steep. Then she dropped in three sugar cubes, which she preferred to loose sugar.

"Any leads on where you might want to work?" Cora asked.

"No. Do either of you have any ideas?"

Jim sipped his tea and stared into the cup. "Chamber of Commerce may be a good place to start."

"We'll send for our grandson to give you a tour of the town in the morning." Cora pulled the tea bag from Stephanie's cup.

Stephanie watched it dangle over the table and plop onto the tray.

"More sugar?" the old woman asked.

She closed her mouth and shook her head. "No, thank you. And a ride isn't necessary. I don't need a chauffeur. I can—"

"We insist," Jim said firmly.

Stephanie sipped her tea and nodded. It wasn't worth upsetting them over something meant to be helpful. "How old is he?"

"Your age."

"Okay. But I am a big girl, despite what my mother probably told you over the phone."

Jim smiled. "He's a good boy. You'll like him."

After a little more chatting, they bid her goodnight, and Stephanie went to bed with a slight headache.

STEPHANIE STRETCHED AT THE TOP OF THE STAIRS and made her way down. She'd slept very little, but at least her head felt better. The house creaked like the House of Usher, and the old windows had whistled every time she was almost asleep.

Near the front entrance was a sitting room lined with bookshelves. In the middle, sat a loveseat and two high back chairs, all facing a coffee table in the center of the room. Old books and dust mixed with potpourri that had long ago lost its pleasant scent.

Stephanie browsed the books, brushing dust from the spines as she went. The shelves were black walnut, with elaborate carvings across the top. She pulled a well-used copy of *Dracula* off the shelf. Her parents had never let her read anything about vampires, claiming they were evil and would poison her mind. If they knew the Nelsons had such books in their house, they'd probably make her move home again.

"Oatmeal's ready," Cora said from close behind.

Stephanie spun to find the woman standing inches away. Heat spread across her face and scalp.

"Ever read that?"

Stephanie shook her head, stuffing the book back onto the shelf.

"A classic, that. Read it a few times myself."

"My parents don't . . ."

Cora smiled. "Some people don't trust their imagination."

A part of Stephanie wanted to defend her parents, but she wanted even more for Cora to back away. "Oatmeal sounds great."

"Ah yes. Getting cold." Cora led her to the dining room, then bustled into the kitchen.

After a few bites of the worst oatmeal she had ever tasted, the sound of a knock pulled her attention toward the front door. "Cora?" She looked over at the door to the kitchen. "Someone's here."

No answer.

Knock. Knock. Knock.

Stephanie went to the entrance, opened the door, and found a man in his twenties staring directly at her. His eyes were a vibrant brown. He moved forward like he might hug her, and his vanilla scent nearly melted her on the spot. She'd been single long enough that she might not have minded a hug, but he backed off.

"Hi," he said.

Stephanie gripped the door. "This isn't my house."

"Course not. It's my grandparents' place." His piercing eyes connected with hers, as if reading her soul.

"Oh. Sorry." She stepped to the side. "I'm—"

"Stephanie, right?"

She nodded and looked closely at him. He was familiar looking. "Did you go to Western?"

"No." He smirked and shook his head. "College wasn't my thing."

"Then how do I know you?"

He raised his eyebrows. "I don't know."

"I grew up a few towns over, in Rutherford. Maybe I saw you somewhere?"

"If you recall, let me know."

"Hey, Eric. Tea?" Cora said, appearing in the dining room.

Eric. The name didn't help her place him. At any rate, he was gorgeous. She admired his worn jeans as

13

she followed him to the dining room.

Stephanie sat quietly at the table, listening to their discussion about family. Apparently, one of their cousins was not well. Sounded like cancer, but she couldn't be sure, as she'd been zoning out on Eric's eyes.

He finished his tea and tapped Stephanie on the shoulder. "Want to ride with me into town? Check out some places?"

Stephanie accepted his offer, then excused herself to get dressed. She dug through every outfit before she decided on a low-cut tank top and her trendiest jeans. She knew she should dress differently to meet potential employers, but Eric seemed more interesting at the moment.

As Stephanie reached the bottom of the stairs, Cora started for the kitchen, mumbling under her breath.

"Nice look." Eric opened the door for her.

She led him out of the house and climbed into the passenger side of his blue pick-up truck. "Nice truck."

"Gets me where I need to be." He started up the truck, turned down the radio—an alternative rock station, from what she could gather—and backed out. "What brings you to my grandparents' house?"

"My mom."

"Don't get along?"

"We get along well enough. She just wants me to

cut the cord, I guess."

"Why is that?"

"I'm done with college. Time to live on my own."

"What did you major in?" Eric focused on the road.

"It was um . . . communications."

Eric nodded. "Better than my not finishing school."

Stephanie felt herself sink into the seat. "Why didn't you finish?"

"Life. My cousin had an accident, and I had to help my aunt and uncle for a bit. They had a hard time with it."

"Is he doing better now?"

"What?"

"Your cousin."

"Oh, yeah. She's on the mend. Should be a hundred percent soon. We hope."

"Can't you go back to college then?"

"No need to anymore. I have a job as an electrician."

"Then why aren't you at work?"

Eric smirked. "Took the day off to help a pretty lady find her way around town."

Stephanie felt a flutter in her stomach. She couldn't remember the last time someone had flirted with her. "Whatever."

"And apparently, she is unaware that she is beautiful."

She felt the deep wrinkles of her dimples crease as she tried to hide her smile.

"Here we are. The Chamber of Commerce." Eric pulled up and parked next to a strip mall. A big green sign advertised *Greendale Chamber of Commerce*. The mall had several shops that Stephanie hoped they'd have time to check out. She loved small town shops. As they exited the truck, Eric's cell rang.

He answered, said "Yup," several times, then hung up. "Boss needs me to check out a service call real quick. You mind hanging here for a bit?"

"Sure, fine," she said in a clipped tone.

"Don't you worry. I'll be back in a few minutes." Eric pulled away.

Chivalry, as it turned out, was still mostly dead. Once inside the chamber of commerce, a woman with long white hair called her over.

"Hi. I'm wondering if you can recommend any places to apply for a job," Stephanie said.

"Yes, of course." The woman pulled a list of businesses from a drawer file. "What is your education level?"

"Bachelor in Communications."

"Do you have a transcript?"

Stephanie felt herself turn red as she fumbled through her purse. "I know I have one." Had she left it at home?

"Regardless, here are a few to try, as they are the only businesses actively hiring at the moment." She circled something on the list and handed it to Stephanie. "The Gray Moon is two doors down. You should start there."

Stephanie glanced at the list of about thirty businesses. Only two names were circled. The Gray Moon and Stein's Grocery. "Thank you."

She left and spotted a wooden sign for the Gray Moon. From the outside, the store looked dark, with black shades over the windows. As she entered, a loud chime rang, and the store clerk popped up behind the counter. A mixture of incense filled the air. Shelves with gargoyle figurines and the like filled the shop. A clothes rack with long dresses and cloaks caught her attention.

"Hello, miss." The man was tall and skinny, with a thick brown beard and long hair. He reminded her of Jesus.

"Do you have applications to fill out for any possible job openings?" she asked, although she doubted she'd apply. Her throat was already sore from the thickly scented air, which made the dull ache at the base of her skull feel worse.

"Are you okay?" the man asked.

"Yes. Why?"

He shook his head. "You look troubled."

She wrinkled her nose and tried not to look annoyed.

"Would you like some guidance?"

She fought back a laugh. Was he selling something?

"All of the new things around you feel familiar, don't they?"

Stephanie stared hard at the man, speechless.

"I can see it all over your face. You're troubled. Uncertain."

"Never mind, I don't want to work here."

He shook his head. "You couldn't anyway."

"What do you . . ."

He motioned for her to continue, but she just stared at his serious eyes. He nodded when she didn't speak. "When you need my help, return."

Stephanie left the shop in a hurry and gulped fresh air once her feet hit the sidewalk. Some people would do anything to make a buck. The incense and whatever else he was inhaling had surely killed some brain cells. Maybe all his brain cells.

She walked back and forth along the sidewalk for fifteen minutes, until Eric finally returned.

He eyed her as she climbed in. "Everything okay?" he asked, and she nodded. "Are you sure? You look bothered."

"I went in a shop, and the dude was creepy."

"The Silver Moon guy? Eh, he's harmless."

Eric spoke so smoothly, Stephanie almost believed

him. Was she being judgmental? No. She had an innate sense about these things. He might not be a serial killer or anything, but he wasn't normal.

Eric pulled into Stein's Grocery and parked. "Let's go and get you a job."

THEY HEADED BACK TO CORA AND JIM'S WITH AN application in hand and a reasonable assurance she would be hired the following day when she returned it. Stephanie would have handed it in already, but she couldn't remember her social security number.

"Gosh. I've written it down a dozen times. Can't believe I forgot it." She shook her head.

"Happens to me all the time." Eric reached across the truck and patted her leg.

She considered grabbing his hand and holding it, but her hesitation caused him to pull away. "How long have you been an electrician?"

Eric looked in the rearview mirror and then back at the road. "Long enough to want a change."

"What else do you want to do?"

"I have prospects on the horizon."

Stephanie wanted to prod him further, but they'd arrived at Cora and Jim's, and Eric exited hastily.

He opened the door for her. "Time to get back to work." He bolted around to his side of the truck and hopped in, waving as he pulled away.

The house was quiet, which suited Stephanie. Cora had left her a peanut butter and jelly sandwich, her favorite, which she devoured as she searched her belongings for her social security card and transcript. She called home and left her mother a message, but didn't get a response.

Later that night, Jim didn't return for supper, so Stephanie and Cora ate alone, exchanging small talk. After dinner, Stephanie went to bed early, hoping to kick her ever-increasing headache, so she could spend some quality time with Eric the following day. Falling asleep on top of her covers, she was awoken by a noise in the neighboring guestroom a few hours later. She sat upright. The sound was faint, like light footsteps, followed by a creaking bed.

Stephanie rolled to her feet and peeked down the hall. Nothing stirred. She tiptoed toward the other guest room, and the bed creaked again. She heard it clearly that time. Stepping into the doorframe, the room glowed just enough from moonlight for her to see everything inside. The bed was empty, the desk cluttered, and the walls covered with clippings and photographs. Shuffling closer, she inspected them. Press clippings were bolded with the words *Accident* and *Miracle*. One article had a photograph of Eric.

A creak in the hallway stole Stephanie's attention. She peeked out but saw no one. She bolted for her own room, locked the door behind her, and pulled the covers over her head. Was she being watched? Maybe the house was haunted. She laid in wait, ready to scream if anyone tried opening her door. But the house was silent, and soon, exhaustion forced her to sleep.

Early morning's white glow welcomed Stephanie to open her eyes. Her blankets were thrashed about awkwardly with the sheets rolled to her feet and the quilt touching her skin.

She eased out of bed and made for the guest room, hoping to get a better look at the articles. When she opened her bedroom door, Cora swept past her toward the stairs.

Stephanie listened for Cora to creak down, but her footsteps had ceased. Was she waiting for her? Stephanie made for the guestroom and heard approaching footsteps immediately.

"Where are you going?" Cora called behind her.

Stephanie found the room nothing like it had been the night before. The walls were empty, save a painting of a cabin on the river. The desk was stacked with magazines and books, but no photograph of Eric and none of the press clippings.

"What happened to all the stuff in here?"

Cora studied Stephanie's face like a foreign word search. "What?"

"Last night, this room looked like a shrine or something. Now, it's empty." Sweat built on Stephanie's forehead.

Cora placed a gentle hand on her shoulder. "You are mistaken, dear."

"This is a joke." She shrugged the old woman's hand away and looked in the closet. Empty. She squatted down and searched beneath the bed. Empty. "I saw it, last night. With my own eyes."

"Must've been a dream, child." Cora smiled meekly, then turned and left the room. "Breakfast in a few minutes."

Stephanie considered the room again. Had she entered a different room? She went to the hallway and looked for another door. Cora and Jim slept in the next room. Beyond that was a closet, and at the hall's end, a narrow door to the attic. This was crazy. Maybe it was just a dream.

"You okay?" Eric stood at the top of the stairs.

Stephanie felt her breath shudder as she looked down at her pink lace pajamas. "Yeah. Just had a dream, I guess."

"What did you see?"

"Some press clippings. One had a photo of you."

She turned a deep shade of red.

"Dreaming about me already, huh?" Eric cocked his head, then broke out in a grin. "Don't worry about it. Old houses always make me dream differently too. Not sure what it is." He motioned for her to follow, then led the way downstairs.

Within moments of Eric's company, Stephanie felt comfortable again. They had breakfast together—another of her favorites, French toast. And before Eric went to work, he promised he'd take her to the grocery store later in the afternoon. Cora and Jim then left her alone all morning.

The restless night had caught up with her by late morning, and Stephanie found herself sprawled on her bed and fast asleep.

She awoke to a gentle rubbing on her back, only to find Eric seated on the bed next to her. "Time to get up, sleepy head."

The moment the light hit her eyes, Stephanie's head pounded at the base of her skull. She squeezed her eyes shut. "I have a horrible headache."

"Uh oh." Eric placed his hand on her forehead. "No fever."

He smelled like a mixture of sweat and fresh linen. Stephanie wanted to turn over and pull him closer, but the moment she opened her eyes, it sent a shockwave through her head.

"Well, can't get a job this way. Let me take you out for the best headache medicine in town."

Stephanie nodded and allowed Eric to lead her out of the room, down the stairs, and to the front door. Eric called to Cora to let her know they were leaving, but she didn't respond. Once in the truck, Eric buckled her in, and Stephanie leaned her throbbing head against the cold window. She'd done this ever since she could remember when she didn't feel well.

Every bump in the road made the throbbing worse. She didn't care what she took, she just wanted it gone. Was this a migraine? It was the worst pain she'd ever felt.

They pulled into a parking lot, and Eric helped her out. She couldn't see the name on the door they'd entered, but she knew where they were, from the strong scent that caused the back of her throat to ache. They were in the Gray Moon.

She halted and felt Eric beckoning her forward. "Why are we here?"

"Only place in town with the kind of medicine you need."

Stephanie wanted to protest, but she wanted to trust Eric even more. It didn't matter what it was—drugs, alcohol, whatever—as long as the pain ended.

The owner nodded in her direction. "Not feeling well?"

"Nope. She needs the good stuff." Eric hugged her and rubbed her shoulder.

After what seemed like forever, the man returned. "Have her sit here."

They walked her to a comfy chair and eased her down. Eric knelt next to her and helped her bring the glass to her lips. "Drink it all the way down. It'll make you feel better."

She took a sip and wanted to spit out what tasted like water from a dog's bath mixed with herbs. She gulped as Eric tipped the glass.

"That's it. All the way to the bottom," the owner said.

Stephanie sucked it down and sunk back into the chair, as Eric took the glass away.

"Hope it's the right mix, Doc," Eric whispered.

"We'll see. She'll need rest now."

Stephanie felt herself losing consciousness. She fought to stay awake. What had she taken? She knew better than to drink anything from anyone she didn't really know. But it was Eric. Cora and Jim's grandson.

"Get her home and wait for me. We'll see if it worked in four hours."

———

STEPHANIE AWOKE ON THE LOVESEAT IN THE SITTING room. She looked above. The ceiling was strewn with spider webs. She looked to the bookcase. All the books looked black with mold.

A loud rap on the door pounded her eardrums. The headache had lessened but was still throbbing at the base of her skull.

"Cora, someone's here," Stephanie called as loudly as she could.

Another knock. What if it was Eric? She placed a hand on the loveseat and attempted to stand. The room swirled. Another knock. She stumbled forward, placing a hand against the wall to get her to the front door. Grabbing the cold handle, she turned and opened.

The outline of a man stood in front of her, but the faint sunlight forced her to close her eyes. "Eric?"

The smell from the Gray Moon. She tried to slam the door.

The man forced his way in. She opened her eyes, and he was inches away, staring her down. He grabbed her shoulders. "Do you know who I am?"

She stared at him for a moment, despite the pain from keeping her eyes open. "You're the owner of the Gray Moon."

The man looked away, clenching his jaw. "You need to come with me." He grabbed Stephanie by the arm and pulled her toward a door. It squeaked on its hinges, and the musty smell revealed where they were going. The basement.

"Cora!" she shrieked.

He forced her down the stairs with far too much force.

"What the hell! What are you doing?"

He pulled her through the darkness, until they stopped along the opposite wall. He flicked a switch in a small room. Light revealed his tear-stricken face. He pointed behind her, and Stephanie turned to see what had his attention. Eric, Jim, and Cora stood behind her. Eric placed his hand on her forehead.

"I love you. Please remember me next time."

"Eric. Help!"

Tears streamed down his face as he pushed her into a room. Inside, there was a bed with straps, and medical equipment, almost like an emergency room safe cell. The man and Eric pushed her to the bed and strapped her down. She fought, but it was no use. Jim and Cora stood at her side, their faces solemn.

Stephanie screamed as a sharp pain pinched her shoulder, then she saw a hand retreat with an empty syringe and a needle dripping with her blood.

"Remember us. We, your grandparents, love you too," Jim whispered.

STEPHANIE OPENED HER EYES TO THE PINK WALLS she'd painted when she was sixteen. Her alarm clock read *10:00 am*. She loved being done with college and sleeping in. Soon, she'd have to find a place to live, but hoped to enjoy Mom's home cooking for a few more weeks. She stepped into her slippers, scuffled down the hall, and found her mom in the kitchen, talking on the phone while tending something on the stove.

"How many more times can we try this?" Mom asked whomever over the phone. "It's not working. It never will. He needs to move on with his life."

"So nice to be home from college," Stephanie announced as she sat on a counter stool.

Her mom startled and glanced at her. "Glad you're home." She hung up the phone.

"Who was that?"

"Marge, from work. Office drama, you know." Mom sprinkled salt and pepper on the breakfast skillet.

"I hope to avoid that when I get a job." Stephanie rubbed a bandage on her shoulder, trying to recall how she'd cut herself.

Mom hung her head. "An old couple nearby will have an open room soon. When they're ready, I think you'll love it. It's in a nearby town. You could get a job there."

Stephanie sighed, annoyed that her mom didn't

trust her to live on her own. She'd been alone at college for four years, living with sloppy roommates. "Mom, is that a new perfume you're wearing? I can smell it over the skillet."

"No. I don't think so." Mom shook her head. "What does it smell like?"

"I'm not sure exactly. It's almost like . . . incense?"

Neighbors from Hell

Karl studied his aunt's dusty photographs displayed along the top of her piano. This was the tenth time he'd looked at them, and still, he couldn't find a clue to her death. The *real* reason, anyway.

The cell phone in his pocket vibrated. He answered it.

"Karl, where are you?" Mom asked.

"I'm at Aunt Jeanie's."

"The house is up for auction next week." She paused. "You might as well forget about your conspiracies."

"I know," Karl replied. "I'll be home before dark."

"Love you."

The phone beeped. His last bar disappeared—*Out of Service*. He pushed the phone back into his pocket and made for the door. The wooden floor creaked beneath each step, sending an eerie bellow throughout the dark and dusty house. Karl pushed open the screen door and strode toward the neighbors'.

Margret, his aunt's neighbor, had been her best friend, at least as far as Margret was concerned. She'd known his aunt better than anyone.

The short path through the forest was already beginning to fill in. Whoever bought his aunt's house next would never even know it existed. Movement on the path caused Karl to stop. Directly in front of him sat a cat. He stepped toward it, and the feline hissed.

"Move it." Karl kicked at it half-heartedly, and it leapt into the woods, disappearing in the underbrush.

Once to her yard, Karl spotted Margret rocking in her chair on the front porch, a cup steaming in her hand. She glanced at him and then into the forest behind him.

Karl picked up his pace and looked back, expecting to see the feral cat, but found the forest to be its normal quiet.

"How are you, young man?" Margret wiped her nose with a handkerchief, and a smile tightened her lips.

"Fine." Karl glanced back at the forest one more time. "Everything okay?"

The old woman nodded and placed her cup on a side table. She folded her hands in her lap and continued rocking. "I miss Jeanie."

Something about the words didn't match her tone. "That's why I'm here." He stepped onto the porch and rested his hand on the graying wooden pillar. "I'm still not convinced her death was an accident."

Margret bit her lip as if she were deep in thought. "I wonder," she whispered.

"Wonder what?" Karl straightened and peered down at her.

"The room in the cellar." Her eyes widened for a moment. "Only place no one has looked, I imagine."

"Never heard of it."

"No, you wouldn't have. Jeanie never showed anyone. Not even to me." She licked her lips. "If anyone could find it . . ." She nodded toward Karl. "You should look in the cellar."

Karl wiped his sweaty hands on his pants. Could something really be hidden in the house? It was unlikely, but worth a shot. This was his last chance. "Is there anything else you could tell me about her? After the sale, I doubt I'll be able to come back . . ." Actually, he *knew* he wouldn't come back. The boonies didn't suit him, but something about his aunt's death had drawn him here. How could a former college swimmer drown? Karl tried to play out something realistic, but every time he pictured his aunt falling into the river, he saw hands shoving her.

Margret shook her head. "I've nothing left to say, except . . ." She looked around, then motioned for Karl to come closer.

He leaned forward, but she beckoned him closer.

The scent of her body odor blended with rank breath.

"Don't take anything. Just tell me what you find," Margret whispered.

"Why shouldn't I? She was my—"

"Some things should not be disturbed." Her voice was sharp, leaving no room for debate. She grabbed his wrist, and her yellowed nails dug into his skin. "Her spirit lingers. Taking anything would only bring wrath."

Karl stepped back. "Her spirit?"

Margret held her finger to her lips and shushed him while looking out into the forest. "She listens even now."

Karl backed up until the railing pressed against him. "I'll leave things as they are." He leapt off the porch and strode away, down the forest path and to his aunt's house. Something about Margret was different. Probably just an attempt by a senile old lady to hide her sadness and keep memories alive.

He went to his car to get a flashlight. Once in the house, Karl made for the kitchen. He opened the creaky door to the cellar and shined the flashlight down the stairs. They were narrow and creaked under each slow step. Karl illuminated the cellar. The floor was a layer of packed, moist dirt, the walls crumbled in numerous places, and the ceiling was a network of solid logs. He hadn't been down here since carrying up an old stove for his mom, and even then, he hadn't come back down to look.

But here he was, and a part of him wanted to forget about it. The police had called her death an accident, and Margret was a crazy old lady. He started on the wall to the left, inspecting the fieldstones carefully as he moved along. Shelves with empty jars showed nothing useful. Moldering wood leaned against the corner. Karl was on his way back up when he noticed something strange beneath the stairs—a large shelf. Behind the shelf hung a dark cloth, large enough for a person to crawl through.

The back of Karl's neck tingled as he bolted across the basement. He shined the light through the shelf. Reaching out, the heavy cloth moved when his hand pressed against it. He knelt and crawled across the bottom shelf, pushing the cloth to the side as he crawled through. On the floor in front of him were bones. He stopped.

The bones were small, from rodents and rabbits maybe. Karl rose to his feet. A shelf on the wall held candle stubs, small skulls, and rocks. The skulls might've been from cats or raccoons. In the corner was a table, and on the table, sat a leather-bound book. Karl grabbed the book. The leather cover felt thick. In the center of the cover was an engraving, *Brystle*. The family name just spelled differently. Karl's mom had said that a hundred years ago or so, the family had switched to the traditional Bristol spelling, and moved to the city. Everyone was surprised when Aunt Jeanie moved back out here. Everyone except Mom, who'd said Jeanie was always happiest when close to nature.

This had to be a family heirloom, maybe a history. Karl opened the book. The words were handwritten and the text was not in English. Had Mom known about this book? She'd never mentioned it. This room would need to be cleaned and emptied before the auction, or whoever found this would probably call the press and say his family were devil worshipers or something.

Karl closed the book and placed it back on the table. Something about this room had to do with his aunt's death, but what? Had someone thought her a witch and killed her? Karl had known her well and had never seen her doing anything strange. This room was probably just a place to house weird artifacts; things she'd found in the woods, like bones.

He shined the light on the shelf. A wooden bowl sat on the top, between a symmetrical spread of candles. Karl removed the bowl. It should've felt dry, but instead, it was moist and tacky. He placed it on the book and peered inside. There were bones. Shiny, white bones that looked like human thumbs.

A shiver traveled up Karl's arms. He reached inside and took a bone. He'd take it home and investigate it. If these were human bones, he'd have to call the police. Despite Margret's warning, he shoved it into his pants pocket.

Karl turned to leave. He'd try his phone again and call Mom. As he turned, the flashlight slipped from his hand and thudded to the floor. It flickered and plunged the room into darkness. The room cooled, and it felt like a breeze had slithered into the basement. Karl's heart thudded against his ribcage, and the blood pulsing to his fingers threatened to shoot from the tips. He crouched and crawled toward the small hole.

His knee caught the flashlight which rolled in front of him and flickered. Something moved in the corner of the room. Karl held his hands in front of him and his scalp tingled. He grabbed for the flashlight, which turned on once he gripped it. He slowly shined the light into the corner. It was empty.

Karl wiped his forehead with his hand before scurrying out of the room. He sensed he was being followed, and raced up the steps, glancing back only when he reached the top of the stairs.

Once outside, he selected his mom from the list of contacts and called her. His phone beeped, and *Call Failed* popped onto the screen. The tower on his phone was at zero. He'd told her he would be home soon anyway. Karl made for his car, taking out the keys as he jogged. He'd left it unlocked, so he flung open the door and jumped in. Breathing deeply, he stuck the key into the ignition and turned. After a few weak engine turns, the start failed. He tried again. Nothing. Had he left something on and killed the battery?

He didn't know shit about cars, but he popped the hood and got out. After propping the hood, he tried the flashlight, which faded to nothing. Then he lit his cell phone to search the engine area for any obvious problems. He looked at the battery and tugged on the wires. All were tight. He pulled other wires and hoses. None were loose. Karl sighed and closed the hood.

The sun was going down over the forest. Soon, darkness would blanket the area.

Margret had to have a phone, right? Karl strode toward her house. He glanced back, and then forward again, scanning the woods for the feral cat. The wind was weaving through the trees and rustling the leaves and underbrush. The path seemed to darken within moments of his entering the forest.

Karl emerged onto Margret's lawn. Light shone from the front porch, and her white hair glowed in the dim light. She stared in his direction as if she'd expected him.

He playfully hopped onto her porch, and she smiled.

"Going to call it a night?" she asked.

"Actually, I was wondering if you had a phone. My car died." Karl held out his hands in a what-do-you-do sort of way.

"Haven't you got a mobile phone?"

Karl held it out. It had a bar. "Actually . . ." He pressed his mom's contact info again, but as soon as he hit send, the screen went blank. He pressed the on button, and the phone remained dead. "Guess the battery's dead."

"Well, I'm sorry, but I haven't got a phone." Margret adjusted her glasses.

Karl felt his shoulders sink. What would he do now? He couldn't sleep in his aunt's house. Not with that creepy room in the basement. If he started walking, maybe someone would give him a lift. No, that wasn't a good idea. It was about thirty miles to town. What if a serial killer picked him up?

"My neighbor has a phone," Margret offered.

Karl looked to the west. There wasn't a house in sight. "I didn't know anyone else lived nearby."

"Oh yes. It's a bit off the road, but you can follow the drive easy enough. Helen is her name."

"Is she . . . friendly?" Karl asked.

Margret nodded. "Like a sister to me and your aunt."

Karl wiped his hands on his pants. "Oh, good. I'll just—"

"Yes, go ahead." Margret shooed him away, then spoke again once Karl turned to leave. "Did you find anything?"

He faced her. "What?"

"In the cellar. Did you find anything?" Her eyes looked sharp.

"Just some junk we'll have to toss before the auction."

"Didn't take anything, did you?"

Karl shook his head and clenched his fists to prevent himself from touching the bone in his pocket.

"Good." Margret picked up her cup and sipped.

Something pierced the air. Like a scream. Karl looked about him, but Margret looked unconcerned.

"Just the wind," she said.

"See you later." Karl shoved his hands into his pockets. He touched the thumb bone to make sure it was still there.

Margret licked her chapped lips. "Better hurry along, before Helen goes to bed."

"Thanks for your help," Karl said over his shoulder.

He crossed the ditch and set foot onto the gravel

road. Part of him wanted to head east and start for home. He didn't know Helen. She might think him a thief. But he continued on until a narrow drive cut across the ditch. It was overgrown along the sides, and a thick line of weeds ran through the center. Karl expected to see lights ahead, but all was dark. Maybe she was already in bed.

Something in his gut told him to turn around, but he was just being a wimp. Soon, he'd be talking to his mother, who'd be here in half an hour.

After about a hundred paces into the forest, a faded white house rose up in front of him. All the windows were dark, save one on the lower level. Karl searched the near sky for phone lines but saw nothing. Had to be too dark to see them. Margret wouldn't lie.

He stopped at the front stairs that led to a porch. Plants that resembled parchment paper hung awkwardly in hanging baskets above the stairs. His forehead warmed. He would've been better off walking home in the dark.

Pressing forward, he climbed the steps and knocked on the front door. After a moment of silence, a hiss came from behind. He glanced back to find the ratty looking cat from earlier, perched on the porch railing. Karl thought he heard footsteps, but he knocked again anyway. Another hiss. This time, from his right. Several cats approached now. A host of them bound from the forest and began making their way up the stairs. The same one who'd met him in the forest hissed again, and its ears pointed back.

The cats were surrounding him. There had to be at least twenty. The door behind him opened and a hand gripped his wrist. Karl yanked away, but the grip was tight. He looked at Helen. He'd expected a frail old woman, but she was broad, with dark hair and a stern face.

"What do you want?" Her tone carried a warning, and her voice was much lower than most women's.

"Ph-ph-phone," was all he could stammer out as he felt the cats close in.

She pulled him inside. "Out of here!" she yelled. The cats scattered before she shut the door.

Karl took a deep breath. "Sorry to trouble you. My aunt Jeanie lived nearby, and when I went to leave her place, my car was dead."

"A young man like you ought to have a cell phone." She stared, like she didn't trust him.

"It died." Karl pulled the phone from his pocket. "Test it if you like."

She considered the phone, before shaking her head. "Jeanie's kin are welcome. Phone is up the stairs and to the left, in the study." She straightened her dress. "Take you up there, if my knees weren't so bad."

"No problem." Karl nodded and started up the stairs. He found a long hall to the left. The first room had an open door. He searched for a light switch but found none. The faint light cast from the hall was enough for him to make out a desk in the center of the room. He felt across the top, and soon his hand found the hard plastic of an old phone. He picked up the receiver. A dial tone. He began to dial until he realized he had no idea what his mom's cell phone number was. Luckily, he recalled her landline, from having memorized it in elementary school. He punched in the number and soon heard a ring. The phone rang six times and then went dead.

He smacked the receiver and listened for a dial tone. A scream pierced the air. It sounded like it'd come from the lower level. Karl raced out of the room. As he entered the hall, something smacked his head, hard. He covered his face and fell to his knees. Warm blood ran over his hands, and his sight darkened. Another whack came from above and split the back of his head open. He lost consciousness.

KARL AWOKE IN A DANK ROOM. HIS HEAD THROBBED, and his face itched from dried blood. Faint light streamed into the small area from a crack in the wall behind him, illuminating the small empty room he was in. A cell full of heavy, musty air.

His attacker had to be Helen. Would Margret come and look for him if he didn't show up? He rubbed the crust from his eyes and peered into the next room through the crack in the wall. When his eyes adjusted, he could make out an empty room with a long table at the center. The table was stained, like liquid had soaked into it many times, and thick leather straps hung beside it.

Karl's body pulsed from his thumping heart, and sweat beneath the dried blood made his entire head itch. He scratched at it, and his fingers became caked and sticky.

Breathing. He heard breathing in the other room.

"Is anyone there?" Karl whispered, but in the still room, it sounded like he'd yelled.

A mat of dark hair appeared, and then an eye. Karl froze, his scalp tingling. The eye stared at him, and the little bit of mouth he could see was smiling.

"You're who they've been waiting for." The woman's voice was soft and sweet.

"Who are you and what the hell is going on?"

"Becca's my name. Hell is about right."

"Seriously. Why am I locked in here? Did Helen do this?" Karl leaned closer to the light.

The squeak of a door stole Becca's attention. "You're about to find out," she whispered.

Through the crack, Karl watched as Helen and Margret crossed the room. *Margret?*

Becca screamed as she was dragged on top of the long table. The leather straps crossed her body, and her hands were tied behind her head.

Margret crossed in front of him, and a door to his left opened, light flooding the room.

Karl stood, his fists clenched. Margret stepped in, a machete hanging at her side. She raised a purple-veined hand, and his knees buckled. He tried to push himself up, but his arms were limp.

"Crawl," she demanded.

"What the hell is going on?" Karl yelled.

The tight smile on Margret's face and her bulgy eyes made her look more like an insect than a woman. "Crawl."

His knees began to shuffle across the floor. He tried to focus on stopping his legs from moving, but they wouldn't listen.

"Stop. I'll walk," Karl whined.

Margret relaxed her hands, and Karl stopped moving. His arms felt normal again. He pushed himself to his feet.

"Don't even *think* about running." Margret gripped

the machete.

He followed her through the door. Becca stared at him from the table, eyes glistening with tears. Her mouth had been gagged, and her clothes looked dirty and ragged. Bones protruded from beneath her pallid skin.

"Sit," Helen instructed.

A chair slid from against the wall and pushed into the back of Karl's legs. He sat.

Karl cleared his throat. "Will someone—"

"—tell you what's going on," Helen simpered. She made a face like a concerned kindergarten teacher.

"Yes," Margret said. "You wanted to know what happened to your aunt."

A cold settled into the room, and the far corner fell into deeper shadow. It felt like ice had formed down Karl's spine.

"You were right, boy. She was murdered," Helen said. "Now we're paying back the coven responsible for it."

Becca squirmed, and a muted scream passed through the gag.

"She did it?" Karl asked.

"Her kin did. And now, we'll use her to bring Jeanie back," Margret said.

"Bring her back? How would . . ." The look in

Becca's eyes told Karl all he needed to know. They would use her body. "But why would they kill Aunt Jeanie?"

"Used bone magic, them." Helen motioned toward Becca. "Jeanie has more power in bones than anyone."

Karl tried to clear his mind of the bone in his pocket, in case they could read minds. But he couldn't stop wondering if Becca could use it to overpower them.

"So why me? What do you need with me?" Karl's voice rose with anger.

"We need your blood," Helen said.

Margret held up a finger. "Not much. Just a prick." She motioned like she was cutting off the tip of a finger.

"And after that, you can go," Helen added.

"Small price to get your aunt back," Margret said.

His entire body cooled, and his hands became clammy. He knew then, he'd never be released. They'd keep him for some foul purposes. Like a slave or something. Or they'd kill him.

The shadow in the corner had grown and sounded like it was whispering to them.

"No more talk. Hold out your hand." Helen pulled a knife from her pocket. The handle was a bone of some kind.

Becca stared at the knife and back at Karl.

Karl took a deep breath and held out his hand. Helen took hold of his right pointer finger and cut a deep slice into the tip. Pain shot through Karl's hand. The dripping blood forced him to look away.

"Squeeze the blood into her mouth," Helen demanded.

Karl walked toward Becca, staring into her deep green eyes. She looked on, staring at his pocket. He pulled down her gag.

"The bone," Becca mouthed, and then opened wide.

He took the bone from his pocket and dropped it into her mouth.

"No!" Helen screamed.

Karl flew into the wall to his right, before being flung onto his back.

Helen plunged her knife into Becca's chest, and Margret hacked at her with the machete.

Becca released a death scream. Karl froze, wanting to help her, but knowing it was too late. He turned and ran. Climbing the stairs, he entered the main level. Becca's screams became fainter as he ran across the main room and out the front door. Fierce hissing filled the outside air.

Cats. They were everywhere. Hundreds of them. They'd been waiting for him.

Everything quieted in Karl's mind. A warmth spread over him as he accepted his fate. *This is the end.* He'd always wondered how he'd feel when his death was near. He'd imagined himself accepting it like a warrior. He wouldn't go without a fight.

Karl charged forward, kicking and swinging his hands over his head. For a moment, he wondered if the cats would part and let him pass. Teeth sunk into his legs. Claws punctured up his sides, front, and back, and it felt as if his scalp might be ripped off. He swung at the attackers, but everyone he knocked off was immediately replaced by another. The weight of the cats brought him to his knees.

Forced to lay face down, Karl closed his eyes. Warmth spread over his body. The stinging pain numbed, and he stopped fighting. He waited for death to take him.

An explosion. Light flooded his vision.

Cats shrieked, and the weight of them lessened. Karl lifted his head and squinted. Through the blood streaming over his eyes, he saw two large objects fly over him and land on the retreating cats. White skin covered in blood—the bodies of Helen and Margret.

Hands gripped his side and rolled him over. A creature stared down at him. It had green scaly skin, with great wings on its back. Karl looked into the eyes. They were deep green.

"Becca?" he wheezed.

The creature nodded. "You will soon pass into the

shadow. Is that what you want?"

Karl sight began to fade. Everything darkened, except for Becca's green eyes. "I don't want to die."

"Then you shall be mine."

As his sight failed, Karl felt himself lifted into the air, followed by a rush of wind.

KARL STOOD NEXT TO HIS MOTHER, AS THE AUCTIONEER peddled an antique buffet table that had been in Aunt Jeanie's dining room.

"I always wanted that," Mother said.

"Why didn't you keep it?"

"Easiest just to split the money." She scratched her cheek. "Uncle Gary is the executor of the will, and this is how he wants it."

After the last of the furniture was auctioned off, the auctioneer began the sale of the last item—the house. At first, there were six people bidding, all of them developers looking for a quick buck. Once it was down to two, Karl pulled the bidder number out of his pocket.

Finally, when the last challenger had given up, and the auctioneer began the call for final bids, Karl raised his number, and the auctioneer acknowledged him.

"Karl, what are you doing?" Mom asked.

Two bids later, the house was his. His mom rested

her hand on his shoulder, and he flinched.

"It's a cash auction. Where did you get that kind of money?" She sounded a mixture of upset and concerned.

"My new girlfriend and I wanted to get a place out here. Thought the house should stay in the family." Karl glanced down at his wrist. Green scales had crept onto the palm of his hand. He crossed his arms over his chest.

"Are you serious?" Mother asked, her eyes wild. "And if you break up?"

Karl forced a smile. "I'll be with her forever."

THE POND'S EDGE

*J*ase wouldn't mistake the eyes of a best friend, and the glowing blues across from him were Alec's. He recognized the black table and the cobwebbed chandelier that cast a faint light, leaving the corners of the room in shadow. He expected Alec to stand and walk away, as he'd done before in this dream. But tonight, something was different.

"Alec, I—" Jase choked on the words. He wanted to look away as tears stung the edges of his eyes, but he was forced to stare at his friend's thick blond hair—shiny and clean, yet unkempt and wild—and his dimpled face, browned from a long-held covenant with nature.

A brief smile was Alec's farewell. But how could he smile, knowing what Jase had done?

Alec's blue eyes were last to fade into the darkness.

Jase woke up and rolled to a seated position on the side of his bed. He wanted to close his eyes, to find Alec again and ask for forgiveness. Maybe then the dreams would stop.

"Time to get up." A woman's voice reverberated

through his flat.

Jase padded across the living room to the slider door, that was left open just enough to let in the breeze. He wanted to lock it and ignore the woman, but instead, he stepped onto the patio.

A woman was seated by the pond. She had a blanket wrapped around her shoulders, with long, red hair straggling down her back. The only redhead he knew was—*no, it can't be.*

He stalked to the pond. The woman rocked back and forth. When he reached her, his heart thumped against his ribcage. It was Alec's wife.

"Sandra, what are you doing here?"

She stared blankly at the pond.

"Is everything okay?"

"Everything will be better soon." Sandra glanced at Jase. "There's been a break in the case."

Jase tried to swallow, but his mouth had gone dry. "Really? Do they have anyone in custody?"

"No. The police don't know anything." Her face tightened with anger and her stare sharpened.

Jase's scalp tingled. "We need to call the police and let them know, so they can—"

"No," Sandra spat. She looked wild—crazy. Her yellowed eyes bulged. Her hair was mingled with bits of leaves as if she'd slept in the forest.

Jase's mind told him to run, but he was frozen. "I don't understand."

Sandra looked behind Jase, and he spun around. He scanned the forest and the pond. At first, he saw nothing, then he noticed large footprints at the pond's edge.

"Look, I didn't mean for it to happen." Jase fell to his knees next to Sandra, covering his mouth with his hands.

Sandra placed a hand on his knee. Her touch was cold. Where her hand rested, his leg tingled, and the chill spread to the ground. Jase tried to stand, but his knees were rooted to the spot as if the mud had turned to cement.

"What the hell!" He wrenched on his legs, but they didn't budge. "Sandra, please let me go. I'm sorry. I'll explain."

She gently placed a hand on his cheek. Cold traveled through his jaw, drilling pain into the nerves. He tried to scream, but he couldn't, and his breathing wheezed.

Slurping footsteps approached from behind. Jase started to shake and imagined Alec's mutilated body. By now it would be white and covered in muck, half-eaten by the pond creatures.

"Alec told me what you did." Sandra's lips touched

his ear, and she pulled him to a standing position. "Now, it's your turn."

Jase was lifted from the ground by a pair of arms. The arms wrapped across his chest were skeletal, with dangling gray skin. The pungent murky water shocked him as he was dragged in slowly. Once in the deep, they plunged below the surface, and everything went dark.

JASE SAT BOLT UPRIGHT AND THREW OFF HIS comforter. The dream had seemed so real. His clothes were soaked with cold sweat. He tore off his shirt as he made for the slider door. He locked the door and peered at the pond, where he'd submerged his best friend's body. This time around, no one was seated near the pond.

He took a deep breath. It had only been a dream. No one knew.

His cell phone rang, and he considered ignoring it, but couldn't, fearing it was business. Last fall, he and Alec had made the biggest score of their lives and nearly got away, but the dealers were well armed. This business had gotten his best friend killed, and maybe soon, it'd be Jase's turn.

"Hello?" he answered.

"Hi, Jase. Can we meet somewhere?"

His heart raced, like it might explode. "Why, what's

up?"

"It's about Alec," Sandra said.

He wiped sweat from his forehead. "Okay." He needed somewhere public, in case his dream had been a warning. "Lunch at Margie's?"

"I'll be waiting for you."

Jase hung up and gripped the countertop with his trembling hands. She couldn't know. This was just another I-miss-him-so-much meeting. Maybe she was lonely.

Jase showered and dressed, and before leaving, decided to pay his respects to Alec. It had been a while since he'd been back there. He strode to the pond, the smell of rotting swamp enough to keep him away after today. Small ripples traveled over the surface, bobbing the lily pads he'd covered this end of the pond with. He'd been told they'd multiply quickly and by-God, they had.

As he turned to leave, he noticed something at the edge of the pond. Footprints.

THE CITY GATE

John Rolle stepped onto the dark street. Sludgy mud and excrement squished beneath his feet. To his left, the northern quarter was a well-lit village all to itself. Snooty bastards wouldn't escape death, but they could pretend for now. To the south, toward the main gate, fires burned as they had for weeks, cleansing the city of the belongings of the sick and dead.

Smoke mixed with the stench of rotting flesh, urine, and shit. John might have heaved if he had anything in his stomach, but the smell was almost becoming normal to him. As he strode into the darkness, he stepped around the corpse of a decaying cat that no one had dared to pluck from the mud. John nearly picked it up, having nothing more to lose.

He passed the fires and leaned against a boarded-up house, just out of view of the city guards, who protected the gate from anyone who showed signs of the pestilence. John waited. Cold and wishing he could stand next to the fire—or in the fire.

After an hour, a boy—who was cursed much like John—approached and halted about ten paces away.

"What's wrong, boy? Afraid I'll infect you?"

"Not you, tough old bastard." The boy tossed a pouch to John. "He approaches the city with a cart of devilry. Should be here within the hour." He pointed at the pouch. "Master Wallen says there's enough to pay the guards a month's wage."

John weighed the pouch carefully. "Half my wage is missing."

"You'll get the rest when the deed is done."

Damn kid knew his business. John considered him a worthy partner, although the boy was not yet a teenager. "Know where I might find a fresh corpse?"

The boy nodded. "Small cottage on the south side of Waverly was boarded up yesterday. The pleas and cries ended this morning. Should be a good one."

Business. That was it. Just business. John motioned for the boy to move on, then strode toward the guards. He recognized one whom he'd dealt with before—Fobs, they called him—but the other, a young pup, was new to the job. John made for the veteran guard, but the young man, a handsome brute up close, stepped in front of him.

"Return to your home."

John cracked a smile. "How's your family, boy?"

The guard raised his club hesitantly. "Why the hell do you care?"

John pulled enough coins to equal the guard's wages for a month and held it out. "This should get them out of the city and away from the devil's pestilence."

The guard's eyes dropped to John's hand, and he gaped.

Without giving the boy a chance to be valiant and reject the bribe, John dropped the coins into his hand. Once a man felt this kind of money, morals were swept away. "Just take a short break when you see me approach. Fobs'll know what to do once my business is done." He handed Fobs his allotment, wondering why the old guard hadn't retired already with all the coin he'd been bribed with.

Both men nodded, and John made for Waverly. The streets seemed coated with the plague as if the mud had slurped up the flesh of the dead and left behind a moist and rotting substance.

John found the small cottage his young partner had described. He pulled a small bar of iron from his belt and removed the well-nailed boards from across the doorway. A door hinge squeaked behind him, and John found a small girl with red curls staring at him from across the street. He gazed at her, wondering if she was alone. Then an elderly man—hopefully her grandfather—pulled her back inside and closed the door. Folk were used to mischief at night when thieves stole from the dead. The Duke's men removed corpses at all hours to purge the county.

The stench was nearly unbearable as he opened the door. In the dark cottage, John could make out a fleshy, half-naked body toward the center of the floor. He'd been an elderly man with a thick beard; his pallid skin covered in blackish welts. The strong rot meant he'd been dead and cooking in the cottage during the sun's peak hours. It wasn't an ideal corpse, but probably the best John would find at this time of night.

He went to work. From his pouch, he removed a jar half-filled with orange marmalade and unscrewed the lid. Then he took a sharpened scraper and chose the largest puss-filled welt. He scraped the rot into the jar and repeated the process three more times. Satisfied, he mixed the jar so well, one might have been able to eat the marmalade on bread without even noticing.

As he returned to the city gate, cries and moans rose from a nearby cottage. Another life claimed.

The guards saw him coming and made their way to a tower meant for their rest or defense if it was needed. Fobs knew his role, so he had placed a pike and helmet where John would see it. John opened the gate and removed the hellish marmalade from his pouch.

With the scraper, he spread the infected jelly over the steel handle of the gate and nearby bolts, leaving a thin enough layer that one would not feel too much tackiness, and the smell would be a pleasant orange instead of death.

With his helmet on and pike in hand, John waited for what seemed like hours. The creaking rumble of a wagon approached. John stood tall, hoping he looked like a proper guard. A man hopped down and stood on the other side of the barred gate.

"I wish to sell the wares of salvation to the survivors in the northern quarter. My name is Peter Wallen."

"Ah, yes. First son of Lord Wallen. I bid you welcome. Please, sir, at your father's request, I must inspect the flesh of your arms before allowing you and your wares to pass through the gate."

Peter Wallen lifted his sleeves and motioned to the gate.

"No, sir. I must inspect in the light. Please, enter the side gate and hold your arms near a torch."

Peter sighed, but hastily opened the gate, wiping his hands on his pants as he rolled his sleeves and held his arms near a torch. "Clean this ghastly gate. Someone has left too much oil or something on the handle."

"I will make sure it is cleaned, sir." John pulled the pin that held the larger gate together and opened the thick wooden doors. "May I ask what you are selling?"

Peter walked his horse-drawn wagon through the gate and opened a chest filled with small bits of dried bread sprinkled with green mold. "Blessed by the archbishop himself and dipped in holy water."

"If ever an item would save the healthy, this is it, sir." John stifled a laugh.

Peter nodded to him, swung himself onto his wagon, and weaved his team between fires and toward the lively quarter.

Once out of view, John dropped the helmet and pike. He held the torch to the handle and bolts where he'd smeared the jelly. A mixture of burnt flesh and orange permeated the air, which stayed with him as he made for his empty home.

As John entered the Gray Lady, a pub on the outskirts of the city, he spotted Richard Wallen tucked away at the corner table.

"Mr. Rolle." Richard motioned to the seat across from him, then sipped his ale.

John took the seat and gulped in a tall porter that had been waiting for him. And a plate of bread and cheese quelled his hunger as he waited for Richard to pay up.

"The rest of your payment will be delivered at

sundown tomorrow. If it worked, you and your family will live handsomely when I become Lord of the estate." Richard sipped his ale. "I expect that to be soon, with my father's failing health and the untimely death of my brother in about three days."

John nearly heaved but fought back the watery acid filling his mouth. "Much appreciated, Lord Wallen."

Richard smirked. Patting John on the shoulder, he left the pub.

John finished his meal and returned home. His was the only home not boarded on the street. He entered and performed his nightly ritual, kissing Claire's cloth doll, holding James' wooden sword, and breathing in the fine scent of his wife, Anne, from her woven shawl that only left her when she was taken to the fires.

Some believed the damned had died from the pestilence. But John knew better. The lucky were gone, and the damned remained.

ANIMAL MEMORIES

The woman seated across the table reminded Rosie of a God, with her wrinkled brown skin, concerned eyes, and her white hair pulled back in a tight bun. Over the phone, she'd sounded hysterical, and now she seemed calm. She'd said the circus was in town for the county fair and that if Rosie was going to help her, it had to be now. Whatever the hell that meant.

"How can I help you?" Rosie asked, half-expecting the woman to breakdown into indiscernible muttering as she'd done on the phone.

"The people there won't help me. They won't say a word, or they'll be next. I know it." The woman curled both hands around her coffee mug and hunched over it like a monkey eating a banana.

"As I said on the phone, I am a law-abiding citizen and won't use evidence gained illegally." Rosie readied her pen to jot down notes. "I didn't catch the location on the phone. Where was your daughter last seen, again?"

"She was at the Rothbury Fair with her friends. She

went to the concessions stand alone and disappeared."
The woman shook her head. "Disappeared right here in
her home town. Police said she ran off with someone.
But not my Rachel. She wouldn't."

Rosie had read every article on the case she could
find, and not a single witness had come forward. Once
people were desperate, they'd seek out Rosie, the
Shadow Investigator. They'd first ask her to help them
out, and then later, if she solved the crime, ask how
she'd done it.

"I charge one thousand for an investigation. Five
hundred now, and the rest tomorrow, if you get results."

The woman tilted her head. "How can you—the
police have been searching for a year and haven't found
a damn thing. Now you expect to find something
overnight?"

Rosie nodded.

The woman pulled an envelope from her purse.
"What's your name again?"

Rosie took the envelope, thumbed through the
bills like a deck of cards, and shoved it into her bag.
"Chances are, you won't want to pay me the rest if I give
you bad news."

The woman shifted uncomfortably in her chair. "I'll
pay you." She forced a smile. "What do you do, exactly?"

"I talk to all the witnesses." Rosie stood and pulled

her messenger bag over her shoulder. "And when I find the truth," she leaned close, so close she could smell flowery perfume, "I seek justice."

Rosie stepped up to the concession stand and watched a young man sweep the floor in preparation for the Circus' big Friday night crowd. "Did you work here last year?"

The young concessionaire looked up and then continued sweeping. "Yeah, third summer."

"God, I remember hearing about that girl. The one who disappeared."

"I don't know nothing about that. Already told the police. Didn't see nothing."

"No, I wasn't asking you about her. I just remembered hearing something on the news. You know how it goes. Hear about something awful today, forget about it tomorrow."

"Yup." He nodded. "Don't even remember what she looked like from the photos the police kept flashing. Too bad though. I remember thinking she was pretty."

"So what time does the circus start tonight?"

"About three hours." After he spoke, the boy began sweeping faster. "People will be pouring in soon and I won't get a break 'til midnight."

"Thanks." Rosie tapped the countertop. "Be back

later for some food."

"I'll be here."

She strode away from the circus concession area. The grandstand was a race track with a large space in the middle, used for everything between concerts and the circus. It wasn't a great circus, but the best one that'd come around here for anyone who enjoyed watching animals submit, or clowns wheeling around with painted-on smiles.

She passed through the fairway, with its deep-fried air and screaming children who wanted something else. She decided to warm up for the night by going to the horse barn. Horses were one of her favorite animals to talk to.

The horse barn was full of teams for pulling wagons, most of them Clydesdales. Rosie petted several, but none seemed inviting enough to talk to. A sign that read *Circus Trolley* hung on the gate of a blonde-maned workhorse named Bunny. The horse smelled sweet, like sweat mixed with oats and molasses. Her pulling partner, Britt, scoffed at Rosie and refused to even face her.

Rosie glanced around for owners, but no one was near. "Here, Bunny." She held out her hand as if to offer a treat. Bunny came near, and Rosie placed her hand on the horse's head. Cold traveled down her arm and out her fingertips.

Share a memory with me. Something that felt wrong?

The horse neighed, and Rosie thought she might be rejected. But the cold turned to warmth, and it spread from the horse, up Rosie's arm, and to her head. She felt it, a dizziness that plunged her into the horse's memory.

We trot through the parking lot, a wagon rolling behind. This has to be the circus trolley. We approach the grandstands from the back. Two men stand beyond the gate. One with a blue cap, and the other with longer hair—a circus performer, no doubt.

The man in the blue cap approaches. He pats us on the head. "Got another sick one I need brought out. A baby elephant."

The memory share ended as the man's face faded to black.

Rosie clung to the horse, hugging its head. It had been weeks since she'd used animal speak, and she felt drained.

"Like that horse, do you?" a man asked from behind.

She opened her eyes and released the link, forcing herself to stay calm, but unable to stop the sticky sweat from coating her forehead. "I just love animals." She rubbed between the horse's eyes—a gentle thank you for sharing the memory.

The man leaned against the gate next to her. She

recognized the blue cap and the scruffy-gray beard. What the horse hadn't communicated was his smell—rotten onion and dirty hair.

"Old Bunny here is one of my trolley horses. Gets to start work soon. Transports the elderly and all that, see."

"Do you run the trolley, then?" Rosie asked with fake interest.

"No," he drew out the word. "I'm head groundskeeper. Lots of responsibility around here during circus and fair week. I'll be happy when racing season starts." He stared at her chest.

"Yeah, I'm sure it's the busiest week of the year. You must have a lot to do. Don't let me keep you." Rosie patted the horse again, hoping he would take the cue and leave her alone.

"You love animals so much, want to come and meet some of the circus animals? I know the ringmaster real well." He leaned closer.

The words sent razors down the back of Rosie's arms, and her scalp tingled a warning. The horse's memory had shown this man interacting with the ringmaster, and it sounded like they had something to bury. Maybe they pretended to have sick animals, but really had human corpses? If she was going to seek justice, she had to play along and figure out what these bastards were up to.

"I'm Rosie. And you?"

He lifted his blue cap. "Frank Patch. Most friends call me Patch."

"I would love to meet the animals, Patch." Rosie walked close enough to make herself gag. She fought the acid creeping up her throat as she took him by the arm. They walked through the growing crowd, who might've thought them a couple. More vomit threatened to fill her mouth.

Patch nodded at the circus ticket booth attendants and walked through. They rounded the grandstands, walked over the race track, and entered a massive yellow and white tent. The inside was abuzz with animal tenders feeding and grooming. A few half-dressed clowns sped around to and fro.

A long-haired, muscular guy—the same from the memory—approached and shook Patch's hand. If he wasn't involved in this, Rosie would've considered dating him. But justice was more important than her defunct love life.

"This is Gerard, the ringmaster," Patch said.

Gerard shook her hand, sending a happy shiver through her body. "Nice to meet you."

"Patch said I could meet the animals."

Gerard's dark eyes twitched, then glanced at Patch.

"Yes, of course you can." He led her to the cage of a huge white tiger. "This is Chloe. She'll not harm you with me here."

Rosie wondered if the tiger might finish her off with one swipe . . . or if maybe, this was how the men killed their victims. Her head would fit in its giant jaws. One shake and a loud snap, she'd be dead.

"What is your interest with animals?" Gerard opened the gate a crack.

"Always wanted to be a veterinarian." Rosie stepped through the thick steel bars.

"I'd better get to work," Patch said. "Have fun, you two."

Rosie's heart pulsed from her ears all the way to her toes. She slowed her breathing and focused on the tiger. "Hi, Chloe. Can I pet you?"

The tiger lay on its side as if it sensed her animal nature. Rosie kneeled beside the cat.

"Loves to have her neck scratched," Gerard said from behind. He'd entered behind her. Was it to protect her or kill her? Sadly, this was often her dilemma with men. Overbearing or threatening.

Rosie scratched Chloe's neck, and the tiger rubbed back like her house cat, Chubs. She focused on the memory sharing, and the cold quickly created the line of connection.

Will you show me what these men do to girls?

Warmth raced back to Rosie's body, and she entered the memory faster than she'd ever done before.

She and the tiger are breathing heavily. Something is being taken from Chloe. Anger forces them to slam into the gate. A cub stands on the other side. Gerard and Patch argue, but the words are unclear. Anger. So much anger fills Chloe that hearing anything isn't possible.

Gerard picks up the cub and hands it to Patch, who smiles from ear to ear. What happens next forces Rosie to close her eyes before seeing it. All she knows is that the cub is dead, and Chloe sinks to the ground with as much sadness as is known to any human.

Rosie fought back tears when she emerged from the memory. Her heart was beating against her throbbing throat. She still hadn't seen anything about the girl, but she knew enough about these two men to hate them.

"Are you okay?" Gerard asked with concern weighing his words.

"She's just a beautiful creature."

"You were like, in a trance or something. Are you sure you're okay?"

"I meditate over the animals. It's how I connect with them."

"Okay." Gerard placed a hand on her shoulder, and she wanted to dive behind the tiger and watch Chloe get revenge for her cub. Rosie would encourage her to seek revenge for her lost cub.

"Want to see the elephants?"

As they left the cage, Chloe growled and began to pace back and forth. Rosie felt bad, for she had pulled a memory into the cat's thoughts and made her relive the worst moment in all her nine lives.

The elephants were separated into stalls and locked behind gates that seemed like a joke compared to a powerful elephant. Rosie moved close to one, but Gerard stopped her. The elephant stared at her with its dark blinking eyes, as if begging her to come forward. Telling her it had something to share.

"Better not get too close to them," Gerard said. "They are mean bastards, these elephants. Only listen to the electric shock or the whip." He cracked a smile and held his whip, like a boy who just caught a snake and was about to show it to his mother.

"They are majestic, though, aren't they?" Rosie asked.

Gerard considered the elephant for a moment. "You could say that." He glanced down at his watch. "Tell you what. How about you come around after the show when they're tired out, and you can get close. Maybe even touch them." He arched his eyebrows and stared at her.

Was this how they'd brought Rachel into their lair? Enchanted her with the animals? Well, that poor girl probably wasn't ready for them. But Rosie was, and she'd sort them out, one way or another.

"Well, thank you. I would love to come back after the circus."

Gerard pulled a ticket from his pocket and held it out to her. "VIP seat just for you."

Rosie took the ticket, gave a fake smile, and walked away.

"I'll have a hotdog and a Coke," Rosie said to the young concessionaire. "Told you I'd be back."

"Yes, you sure did." He glanced at Rosie's chest. "Five dollars, please."

She handed him the money and took the hotdog and Coke from the counter.

"Do me a favor?" the young man asked.

Rosie nodded.

He handed her another hotdog and pointed to a German Sheppard trotting down the fairway toward them, weaving through the crowd. "Feed old Hunter for me. Boss doesn't like me feeding him."

"Sure." Rosie took the hotdog and called for Hunter. The dog paused, perked his ears, and walked toward her slowly as if stalking her. She unwrapped the hotdog and held it out for him. The dog took the food gently, huffed it down in three bites, and trotted away.

"Poor boy. Should take him with me when I leave."

"Why do you say that?" Rosie asked.

"His owner is um . . ." The boy glanced up and then quickly back down as he took a hand towel and wiped down the counter.

Rosie turned to find Patch leaning against the side of the concession stand.

"Hey there." He placed a hand on her shoulder. "My seat's next to yours. Can't wait for the circus to start." His smell was worse now, as he'd tried to conceal his stink with cheap deodorant.

"Thanks for the food, young man," she said.

The concessionaire continued working hastily. Patch glared at the boy like he wanted to cuss him out.

"Circus starts in half an hour. Lead the way," Rosie said.

The grandstands were half full when they took their seats in the reserved section. A young woman checked their tickets and looked from Patch to Rosie, staring Rosie in the eye longer than a casual glance. Patch placed a jacket on his seat and said he'd be back after checking in with the other groundskeepers.

Rosie ate her plain hotdog, pink and fleshy, like a pickled finger, then sipped her Coke. Footsteps shuffled and skidded across the bleachers, and a haze of sweat and too much perfume hung in the air. Directly in front of her was the asphalt race track made into a stage with a large portable curtain behind it, blocking the view of the yellow tent entrance.

Patch returned with a red slushy for her. "Red is my wife's favorite."

Rosie looked at his left hand. Sure enough, he wore a gold wedding band on his ring finger. She sipped her slushy. It tasted like fake cherry mixed with cold plastic.

"How long have you been married?"

"Twenty years this September. Loves the month of September, my wife."

"Why isn't she here at the circus with you?"

Patch adjusted his blue cap and stared ahead. "Doesn't care for the tigers. Scare her, those big cats."

Rosie had touched a nerve. Maybe his wife knew he was bad and couldn't leave him, but still refused to be around him in public.

Music began over the intercom—trumpet music as if announcing the entry of a king. At a proper circus, this would be a live band, but here, in the Rothbury grandstands, music over the intercom was as good as it got.

Clowns streamed from the tent, bouncing, cartwheeling, and riding unicycles. In groups, they took massive slingshots and launched rolled-up T-shirts into the crowd. Then, at last, they replaced the T-shirts with water balloons. One splattered just below Rosie and droplets of warm water streamed down her bare legs like small trickles of blood.

Patch chuckled and pointed at the stage. Clowns on camels rode out and pretended to race around. One fell and sprawled on the ground, causing much of the young crowd to laugh. The next act was a pair of sweater-wearing poodles who performed tricks and received twice as many cheers as the clowns and camels.

Gerard followed a cage onto the stage and Chloe was released. Rosie could've sworn the tiger glanced at her and did a double take. She would've loved to take that big cat home. Chloe was impressive, jumping through hoops and leaping over obstacles. She retired almost cheerfully to her cage—the most unnatural home for a giant cat.

Finally, the elephants—five in total—marched onto the stage to the beat of music. They walked on two legs for a lap. One even climbed on top of the other two to form a small pyramid. Only cruelty would train such powerful creatures.

"Well, it's almost over. Better get back to work. Nice sitting with you." Patch glanced at the slushy in her hand. "Don't let it go to waste." He tipped his blue cap and descended the stairs. At the bottom, he waved and left.

Rosie wanted to drop the slushy to the ground below but worried she might ruin some kid's night by showering him in red.

When it was all over, she followed the crowd out, stopping at the concession stand to toss her full slushy and buy another drink. The young man glanced at her and then ignored her. "He's watching. Get the hell away."

Rosie felt her forehead warm. She still needed to see more memories to have any proof that these men had killed Rachel. So far, they were guilty of animal cruelty, which was enough to condemn them in Rosie's mind. The elephants might be a good source. If she could find the German Sheppard, Hunter, he'd be the best.

Rosie nodded and made for the entrance to the race track. She followed a path to the tent where she'd met Gerard earlier. A cluster of clowns stood in a circle, most of them smoking. They eyed her as she approached.

"Gerard said I could see the elephants," she explained her presence to a small, red-haired clown whose make-up was sweating off so badly it made it look like her face was melting.

"Get out of here," the clown spat.

"Rosie, dear," Gerard called.

At the sound of his voice, the clowns dispersed, several giving her creepy looks with their painted-on smiles and sad eyes.

"The elephants are not fit to be seen tonight." He stepped close to her and took her hand.

Rosie pulled away, and adrenaline shot through her veins. "Don't touch me."

Gerard held up his hands. "Not so friendly."

"I don't like to be touched." Rosie reached into her messenger bag and gripped the dagger she carried for protection.

Gerard stared at her in silence, his thorny eyebrows shadowing dark eyes. "I let you pet Chloe. Counts for something, doesn't it?"

A low growl sounded from somewhere in the tent. Rosie wanted to release the tiger and run. Chloe would surely protect her. Instead, she turned and strode toward her car.

"Wouldn't have been a very good lay anyhow," Gerard called.

Rosie clenched the dagger and continued forward. *Patience. Patience.* He'd get what he deserved. She made for her car, glancing back to see if Patch was following. If she would've messed around with Gerard, she'd probably be dead already. She reached her car door and

82

as she went to unlock it, two glossy eyes, not ten feet away, caught her attention.

A whimper. It was a dog. Hunter crept toward her and sat on his haunches as if inviting her to communicate. Occasionally, an animal could sense her instincts, but it was rare.

Rosie placed her hand on the dog's head. She focused with everything she had, and the cold that she'd never get used to traveled down her arm and to her fingertips.

Will you show me something?

Nothing happened right away, and then the warmth overtook her body, and everything faded to black.

She watches through Hunter's eyes as Rachel runs from Patch. He calls for the dog to help him, but Hunter remains seated. When Patch catches Rachel, he throws her to the ground. He drags her back to the tent where the dog stands in wait. Rosie can sense the dog's concern now—breathing heavily and wanting to attack.

Patch reaches for something next to Hunter and the dog nips. Patch takes a baseball bat from the side of the tent and smacks the dog on the head. He then pulls Rachel to her knees and knocks her out cold with the bat. Taking hold of her feet, he drags her body toward the woods.

Hunter follows close behind. Within the forest is a run-down house with an exterior door down to its basement.

Patch removes a key from beneath a rock, unlocks a padlock, and brings the body below.

Rosie emerged from the memory, heart pounding so hard, she feared it might explode. Sweat ran down her back to form a cold blotch on her spine. Hunter shook off her hand and padded away. Rosie had enough to go to the police. If she remained on the premises and tried to find the abandoned house, she might be the next body buried below. That had probably been their plan all along.

She held the car door handle for a long moment before releasing. Many cars had left the parking lot. If she remained too long, her screams might go unnoticed. She had to act now. Rosie bolted down the road that led behind the race track. She searched the forest for an opening, and with little trouble, found one.

The abandoned house was only about twenty paces from the edge of the forest. She pulled a small light from her purse and searched for the entrance to the basement. The house itself was moldering, with the windows broken and shattered. The roof had caved in over nearly half the house. In back, she found the cellar door. The rock and the key were right where Hunter had remembered. Rosie stuck the key into the rusted lock, and it opened with a squeak.

She set it aside and pulled the doors open. A cold,

rotting smell wafted up from below. Rosie shined her flashlight onto the uneven concrete steps that were chipped and blackened. When she hit the bottom, the scents of decay and rot strengthened. The room was small and empty. To the right, a doorway. She shuffled toward it and pushed aside the tattered sheet blocking her way. Shining her light into the next room, she saw corpses. Some were clothed skeletons, while others were covered in rotting flesh. The sight brought vomit to the top of her throat. Most were laid awkwardly on chairs and musty furniture. Across the room was a bed, and in front of the bed were the bodies of animals.

Rosie stepped over bones on her way to the bed. It was neatly made and adorned with a fully dressed skeleton on top of the quilt. The skeleton's left hand was on top of its heart, a diamond ring gleaming from the rays of the flashlight. Patch was married. And here was his wife.

Noise sounded from outside. Rosie began to panic, to the point where breathing became difficult. She was trapped. The outside doors squeaked open. She dove behind an old dresser and extinguished her light. In the dark, she heard someone enter, dragging something in the dirt.

A low moan. The victim was still alive.

Within ten paces, they stopped.

"I told you not to talk to anyone or to feed that damn dog," Patch said, and a painful groan was the only response. "Now, you will keep Monique company."

A final moaning response was cut off by a loud snap of bones breaking.

Rosie tried to control her breathing; tried to stop her heart from pounding so loudly. She might as well call out to him. Might as well give up. Maybe someone would investigate if she disappeared too. Maybe not.

A light shone in front of her. She glanced down. Her own light was still off. She looked up, only to find cold eyes boring into her own.

"You should have left when I gave you the chance."

"What the hell are you talking about?" Rosie gasped.

"The slushy would have made you ill. Made you leave for home. Now, you've seen too much."

"But I won't—"

"Ah, but you will." He glanced toward the bed. "I had to do this. She was taken from me by a tiger. She needs company for when I'm gone. You'll love her, like all the others." Patch gestured to the room at large, then stared at Rosie before reaching for her.

Rosie pulled the dagger from her purse and stabbed it through his hand. He recoiled in pain, and she shot for the door. She made it halfway up the stairs before he grabbed onto her heel. Shaking her leg free, she trudged up the stairs and into the night.

Hunter sprinted from the forest and plowed into Patch, who threw the dog into the side of the house. A loud yelp was all Rosie heard as she ran.

Patch was right behind her. She sprinted toward the circus tent. The only people left here might be tending the animals. She needed help.

Once in the dark tent, she searched for someone. Anyone. It was as if everyone knew to leave after the show, to stay away from Patch. They knew he was bad. A murderer. And none remained at the circus tent. A loud growl caught her attention. Chloe!

Rosie ran for the tiger cage. She shuffled her fingers over the wall next to the cage for keys but found nothing. Chloe growled. Rosie looked back. Patch was fast approaching with a pitchfork in his hand. She ran.

A bellow caught her attention. The elephants. She ran toward the stalls and climbed over the gate of the big one who'd stared at her earlier. The elephant forced her to touch him and after a flash of cold, then heat, it brought her into a memory.

Rosie watches through the elephant's eyes as Patch ties up and leads a newborn baby elephant out of the tent. A primal scream blares from the mother elephant.

The world appeared around Rosie again. Patch was

lowering himself over the gate.

"Step aside, you old cow," he said to the elephant.

Once within range, the elephant knocked him over and with one stomp, crushed his legs. Patch lay there screaming, and Rosie smiled down at him.

"Justice."

She pulled handcuffs from her bag and slapped them over his bloody wrists. Then she pulled out a gag, stuffed it down his throat, and tied a cloth over his mouth. The elephant smashed open the gate for her, and with all her might, she dragged Patch toward the abandoned house in the woods.

"BEFORE WE MEET, I WANT YOU TO KNOW, I AM A law-abiding citizen and won't use evidence gained illegally."

"Okay. When can we meet?" asked the man on the other end of the phone.

"I work until six. I'll call you when I'm done." Rosie hung up and pulled her binder from her briefcase. She rolled down the windows to air out the car, which smelled like wet dog—Hunter needed a bath tonight. She got out of her car and went around back, opening the trunk. She grabbed her medical bag, ready to provide hospice care to old Betty Lynn who was rotting away inside the white house before her.

Rosie glanced at the small pile of necklaces, figurines, and other trinkets shoved in the corner of her trunk. There were seventeen in total. Seventeen solved cases where justice was served. Next to the pile was her new favorite nostalgic item, a blue cap.

About the Author

J.R. Roper is the author of the Morus Chronicles, a fantasy series for middle grade readers. The Hunter Awakens, The Spirit of Steel, The Tower Below, and The Silver Spear are now available along with a collection of short stories titled Mel & the Black Rider. Roper's work has appeared in ChildGood Magazine, Families First Monthly, and in anthologies by Crushing Hearts and Black Butterfly Publishing, Horrified Press, and Thirteen O'Clock Press. His essay, Over The Edge, was published in Imagine This! An ArtPrize Anthology Volume 3, and nominated for a Pushcart Prize.

Awards include a 2017 Children's Literary Classics Award, 2016 Moonbeam Award for best series, a Foreword Reviews 2015 IndieFab Book of the Year Award Finalist, a 2015 Children's Literary Classics Award , 2015 Readers' Favorite Gold Medal Award for Children's Action, and the Best Children's Novel of 2014: Preditors & Editors Readers' Poll.

For strange tidings and to receive a FREE ebook of Mel & the Black Rider visit:
http://joerroper.com

Thank you for reading. Follow your passion.

Author J.R. Roper

Photo Credit: Debbie Hall Photography

WWW.JOERROPER.COM